THE BILLIONAIRE'S CHRISTMAS BRIDE

L. NICOLE

The Billionaire's Christmas Bride

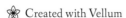 Created with Vellum

Nikolai Serepova took one look at Gabriella and knew he had to have her. He was too old for her, but it was like lightning struck him when she smiled and there was no way he could walk away. He's been biding his time and finally, the moment is right. He has Gabriella right where he wants her. He's going to claim her and nothing will stand in his way.

Billionaire Bad Boys are just what the series title implies. They're filthy rich, and well, just plain filthy in general. They know what they want and when it comes to women, once they find 'the one' there's no way they will walk away. If you like safe reads with insta-love, Alpha men, and a definite happily ever after, then you're in luck, because that's exactly what's inside a L. Nicole book.

1

GABRIELLA

His eyes are one me again. I can feel them despite the crowd between us.

I take a sip of my champagne. That's probably a mistake, because I'm a lightweight when it comes to alcohol, but I always hate these parties. I wouldn't be here at all, but my father demanded my presence. When George Hawthorne the Third requests you show up, you just do it. You don't ask, you don't try to deny him. If you do, he'll make you pay for it. My stepfather is really good at making you pay. He's made my mom pay every day for marrying him.

At the thought of the pain my mother suffers at his hands, I take another drink. My mother and I aren't close, and I will *never* be anything like her, but I hate how she chooses to live. She sold her soul to the devil—the devil being step-daddy-dearest. She knew what she was doing, but she was tired of living without money.

I shouldn't complain about that. After all, I get a sweet little allowance every month. I'd give it up tomorrow, however, if it meant I'd never have to see George again. Since that's quite clearly never going to happen, I figure it's a just payment.

These parties are usually the bane of my existence. Rich, snobby people, all pooled together in one place, playing I have a bigger pocketbook than you. I nod, smile, and appear the loving stepdaughter for photos when I have to. Then, I leave as soon as I can.

I stare up at the clock, because I know that option isn't going to be available until I make it through this dinner. I walk outside on the balcony overlooking the grounds, needing a moment of fresh air before I have to go place nice with George and Mom. There are times when the urge to run away becomes so strong that I can think of nothing else. But, the truth is, there's no running away from my life. George keeps a tight leash on all aspects of his life and that very much includes me.

I look out, the air cool, but it is almost Christmas. We live too far south for snow, and that makes me sad. Maybe a blanket of crisp, white snow would help disguise the ugliness of the people gathered here. I watch as they mill about the courtyard, so freaking pretentious they stink of it. They're all alike. Every last, single one of them are just like my stepfather and mother.

With the exception of one man.

Nikolai Serepova.

He's unlike anyone here. In truth, he's unlike any man I've ever met before. He's a lethal combination of sex and sin. Shrouded by darkness so mysterious that you're drawn to it, even knowing that if you get too close it will kill you.

That's why I steer away from him. I have enough problems in my life, without courting the danger that is Nikolai. I'm not stupid, and I know that playing it safe is the best way to navigate this world that I live in.

Except tonight I'm not safe.

Tonight I'm in more danger than I could ever explain and all because I caught his eye.

Even now, I feel the heat of his stare hitting my back, warming my skin despite the distance between us. I feel my heartbeat speed up in reaction. I'd be lying if I said Nikolai doesn't excite me.

He does.

I think Nikolai has the power to excite every woman from sixteen to eighty. Maybe it's because of that hint of danger that is draped over him like a second skin, or maybe it's just that he truly is beautiful. He stands well over six feet, has jet black hair that is wavy and unkempt, but in a way that it looks like it's had a lover's hand brushing through it for days. His eyes are black as midnight and so intense that you could drown in them. His body is impressive, filling out his perfectly tailored suit in a way that makes a woman go weak in the knees, imagining what he looks like underneath it. Then, there is his accent.

He speaks perfect English, but his accent makes the words sound like poetry slipping from a lover's tongue.

Not that I've ever experienced this directly. I've only heard it from a distance, preferring to keep safe in my little bubble. Still, the temptation to reach out and tempt the devil to play with me has been there.

But, I've ignored it.

Wisely ignored it. Much like I'm doing right now. I will my heart rate to fall back to normal. I'll get through dinner and do my best to charm whatever bored businessman that my stepfather is trying to con out of his money, flash my cleavage when the opportunity arises, cross my legs and sound hopelessly inept. I'll play my part and ignore the heated stare from the one man I want and shouldn't. And then...

Then, I will run back to my safe little apartment. Far away from men like Nikolai Serepova.

2

NIKOLAI

She's meant to be a distraction.

And it's working.

I saw the way my adversary spoke with her, hurriedly, stilt-edly, in the corner. His hand capturing her wrist and holding it much too tightly. I saw the look of pain flash over her features before she hid it from view, replacing the hurt with a look of cool aloofness that intrigued me. She hates her stepfather. That much is completely obvious. Still, she is here, playing her part.

What is her motivation?

Money?

I can understand that. In my experience, most people are elemental, reacting on one fundamental rule.

Money makes the world go around.

Everyone has a price. It's just a fact.

Still, the woman teasing me in that golden, nearly see-through, dress—that is too short to be decent and too long for my liking—is a mystery to me. One that I can admit I definitely wish to unravel.

This isn't the first time I've noticed Gabriella Alvarez. Hell no.

Not even close.

I've made a pastime out of getting to know her. I have a folder locked in my desk that is full of her basic information.

Age?

Twenty-one. Young, but definitely legal.

Name?

Gabriella Marie Alvarez. Named after her grandmother.

Parents?

Heather Mayes Alvarez Hawthorne and Thomas Alvarez. The couple was married for ten years until Heather left Thomas, a landscaper in Southern California, for one of his employers—one George Hawthorne, a man ten years Heather's senior and with a soul so black that it almost makes mine look white.

Apparently, Heather has a very elemental price, one she accepted, even if it meant marrying the devil to achieve it. She wanted to be rich. She achieved her dream, but I wonder if she liked the way that turned out.

Is her daughter so easily swayed?

If I threw a couple of million her way, would my little pretty dance for me the way I want her to?

The idea intrigues me, not that it is material.

I want Gabriella. I haven't been watching her, studying her, and making plans for the last year without a purpose. I have her stepfather by the balls and to get free he's going to give me the one thing he has that I want.

Gabriella.

He just doesn't know it yet.

3

GABRIELLA

"You look... *cold*."

Of all of the ways I imagined Nikolai Serepova approaching me, this wasn't it. His hand settles against my bare back and immediately my body stiffens in response. It feels as if electricity explodes inside of me, making me quake and my legs feel unsteady.

"What makes you say that?" I ask, amazed that my voice doesn't betray my nervousness. I turn to face Nikolai and the first thing I notice is that he is even better close up. Not that I think that's a good thing. I shouldn't be in Nikolai's private space. He chews women up and spits them out.

"Perhaps the fact that I can see your ass through the fabric of your dress," he responds quietly, his Russian accent as beautiful as the rest of him. It almost sounds like he's chastising me, which I find curious, but steadfastly ignore.

"It's an illusion of the fabric," I tell him, with a small grin. "Trust me my ass is safely hidden."

That's mostly the truth. The fabric is sheer, but the glittery underlay is black, but made of lace so it is a somewhat transparent. You don't see the skin of my ass, but you definitely see the outline and the fabric is definitely clingy.

"Trust me, there is nothing hidden," he retorts and as if to prove his words his hand slides down my back to cup my right cheek.

"You should move your hand," I warn him, my throat suddenly dry.

"I happen to like where it's at," he counters, and for some reason it almost feels like we're in a tug of war, a matching of wits and I have a very bad feeling Nikolai will devour me. "Sometimes the landscape is so beautiful that it must be protected as well as admired," he adds and I ignore the quiver that sends through my heart, or the beat it seems to skip because of it.

"But, I don't like where your hand is and the last time I checked, I'm still the owner of this particular landscape, Mr. Serepova."

"Nikolai," he says, still not moving his hand.

"I should be going. My stepfather will be wondering where I am," I tell him, excusing myself. My heartbeat quickening as I look into his eyes. I've heard the others talk about Nikolai Serepova as being ice cold. They say he has no emotions whatsoever, that he is cold, calculating and strikes without warning. All I feel is heated and that heat is reflected in his eyes.

There's definitely nothing cold about him right now.

"Do you always do what your stepfather demands of you?" he asks, clearly ignoring my attempt to leave.

"Only when I have no other choice," I tell him truthfully, even though I probably shouldn't.

"What are his demands tonight, Gabriella? Are you here to distract? Get the sheep to invest in George's latest scheme?" His voice sounds so bored and cynical. Then again, he has my stepfather pegged, so he has a right to be cynical.

"I have no idea what you mean," I respond with an easy shrug.

"Don't lie to me, Princess. I don't want lies between us ever."

His words feel heavy, weighted and they make my heart and imagination run away with me. I shake my head to clear it.

"There's nothing between us, Mr. Serepova," I deny.

"Now, I think we both know that's a lie, don't we, Princess?"

"Why do you call me that? I don't like it," I tell him and I think I feel fear blooming in my chest, because I don't miss the gleam that flashes in his eyes. The last thing I need is for Nikolai Serepova to picture me as a challenge.

"Because you are regal, made to be a princess. In fact, I'm going to make you *my* princess."

"You can't make me anything, Mr. Serepova."

He studies my face and I have the strangest sensation that he finds me amusing.

"We'll agree to disagree, sweet Gabriella," he says and maybe I should breathe easier at his easy acceptance. Except, his hand begins moving up my body, his fingers grazing over my dress and skin are light and teasing, but they feel like pure heat wherever they touch. I don't speak—I barely breathe—as his hand somehow makes its way slowly from my ass to my neck. Then, his thumb is sweeping gently back and forth across my cheek, his eyes growing so dark they look like liquid. There's this connection between us, an undercurrent that I've never experienced before and I have a feeling I never will again, at least with anyone but Nikolai. My body feels alive, my mouth dry, the inside of my thighs damp with excitement and goosebumps are scattered across my skin. I lick my lips, swallowing as I try to find my bearings. I need to walk away. I'm on dangerous ground here.

"Dinner is starting," I murmur, unable to grasp any other words. I have no idea if they are really starting dinner, but it's an excuse and I'm going to take it. I move to turn away, but he tightens his hold on my neck, his thumb still stroking my skin.

"You want me."

Three little words. Three words coming from his deep voice that make it even harder to breathe.

"I don't," I refute, not wanting him to know the truth.

"Your mouth denies it, but your body proves you a liar, Gabriella," he says.

"I don't know what—"

I stop talking when my gaze follows his as he looks down at the front of my sheer dress. Clearly my hard nipples are swollen, distended and on display. I really should have thought twice about this dress tonight.

Before I can say anything, maybe even run away screaming, Nikolai surprises me by whisking off the jacket to his suit and draping it over my shoulders.

"What are you doing?" I ask him, holding the jacket together to hide my breasts and doing my best to ignore how it feels to be enveloped in Nikolai's cologne. Good Lord, it should be against the law for a man to smell this good...

"Hiding what is mine," he says and it feels like my stomach drops at his proclamation. I've not only caught Nikolai's attention, I have a feeling I'm not getting away from him...

4

NIKOLAI

"I hope my daughter isn't bothering you, Nikolai," George says.

He sounds like he's joking, with a fake smile plastered on his pale face. But, I don't miss the look of censure he throws Gabriella. I also don't miss the way her body tightens as we approach him. I've rolled the sleeves up on my jacket to make her comfortable, but also made sure her body was no longer on display. Some things a man wants to keep to himself.

My hand is on her back and I keep it there, partly because I want to stay connected to her and want her to get used to my touch. Mostly, I want to remind her that she's not alone. I don't like the idea of Gabriella being intimidated by anyone.

"Not at all, your stepdaughter is quite entertaining George."

I keep my voice cordial, it's taken years of practice to keep my irritation and anger from showing. I manage it quite well these days, but with Gabriella involved, it's definitely testing my limits to talk with this idiot.

"She has her uses," he laughs. "In fact, I was just telling Stanford here that you're attending the university and majoring in economics, Gabriella. That's what Stanford specialized in and he's made quite a name for himself," George says. "You two should have a lot in common."

My hand on Gabriella tightens in reflex.

The old bastard.

He knows what he's doing. There's no way in hell she has anything in common with Stanford. I might be older than Gabriella, but Stanford is at least sixty.

"Is that so?" Gabriella replies, her voice lacking any of the fire it had when her and I talked earlier. It sounds dead and I instantly hate it.

"It is. I'd love to spend some time getting to know you, Gabriella," Stanford says, and I move so that my body is between the two of them. If Stanford thinks for one minute he's getting his hands on her, he needs to think again.

"Let's retire to the grand dining room," George interrupts, probably picking up on the tension, since he casts a worried gaze in my direction. He should be worried. *He should be very worried.* "There are some men I'd like to introduce you to, Nikolai. I've taken the liberty of seating you with them. They wanted to talk to you about your shipping business. Gabriella give the man his coat back and you can show Stanford how to find the dining room after giving him a tour of the courtyard. I was telling him how you took lead in the design. Not sure why you borrowed a jacket anyway. It's hotter than hades here," he mutters and I feel the finest of tremors move through her body.

I don't know what their relationship is, but it is clear George thinks he has his stepdaughter under his thumb and it's even clearer that Gabriella not only dislikes him, she's afraid of him as well.

When she begins to take my jacket off, I put my hand over her arm, refusing to let her.

"I'm afraid, gentlemen, that Gabriella and I already have plans," I announce, moving so that my arm is around Gabby's body, resting on her side as I pull her against me. She goes so stiff that I'm sure it has to be painful. I rub her hip comfortingly. "Relax," I murmur against her ear, where only she can hear me. Although I don't give a damn if the others do. They need to realize that Gabriella is mine now. I've been biding my time and now, finally, the wait is over.

"Plans? What plans? Gabriella never mentioned any plans. Nikolai, I know you are used to getting your way, but I'm afraid Gabriella has obligations—"

"You're right, she does have obligations. She agreed to fly to Karpathos with me for the Christmas holiday. We leave tonight," I announce.

This time, Gabriella gasps, turning to look at me like I am insane. She doesn't argue with me, however. Instead, she just looks confused, which is understandable.

"Now, see here, Nikolai—"

"Perhaps you and I should speak, George."

"We definitely should. I don't know—"

"In private," I tell him, my voice firm, and the censure in my tone is unmistakable. I can air all of his dirty laundry here, but for Gabriella's sake, I find myself hoping he doesn't make me. George studies me and this time I don't bother hiding my displeasure.

"Perhaps, we should," he responds and it brings me a hell of a lot of pleasure to see the fear in George's eyes this time.

"I think maybe—"

Before Gabriella can back out, or cause more trouble for me, I turn her to face me. "Go pack an overnight bag, Princess. I'll be up to get you in a moment."

"What are you doing?" she asks, and I can see that she's wrestling with herself.

"Your life is about to change, Gabriella. Now go upstairs and pack an overnight bag," I instruct.

It doesn't really matter to me if she packs an overnight bag.

THE BILLIONAIRE'S CHRISTMAS BRIDE   13

She will have all new clothes and jewelry, anything she needs. I want it to come from me, not from money her stepfather or mother have given her. I will be the one to take care of Gabriella from here on out.

Just me.

For a moment, I think that she might argue with me. Then, she surprises me my nodding her head in agreement. I kiss her lightly on the forehead in praise. She pulls away from me and walks toward the stairs. She's beautiful, but I feel the urge to rip off my shirt and beat at my chest when I watch her wearing my jacket, knowing that I've claimed her as mine and that soon she will be mine in every single way.

5

GABRIELLA

"What have I gotten myself into?"

I'm alone in my room, so I'm asking the question to no one, really.

Just myself.

The problem is that I don't know the answer. Somehow, I've managed to catch Nikolai's eye and he's stepped in and I have the very real fear that he's going to take over my life, I just don't know how I feel about it.

I sit on the bed. I'm supposed to be packing, but I'm not really going anywhere.

Am I?

If Nikolai gets his way, and I have no reason to doubt he will, am I really contemplating going to Greece with him for Christmas? That would be insanity. I don't know him. I'm not even sure I like him.

But my body does.

There's no point in denying that. I've never been the kind of girl to run away from things, and I'm not about to start now.

I want Nikolai Serepova.

I like the way he makes me feel. I like the tingles of awareness that move through my body anytime he looks at me and I love the way he touches me, even lightly. It has a degree of ownership in it that I should rail against, but I like it.

I even think I'd like to belong to Nikolai. That sounds crazy, but it's true.

Still, going through with this is not without complications that could be huge. This will piss George off. Since he married my mother, I've done everything I can to keep that from happening. If it was just me, I could probably deal, but I've always tried to protect my mom. It's not that she deserves it, but something inside of me says that's what I'm supposed to do—even if it doesn't make any sense.

If George is upset, and me leaving with Nikolai will definitely make him upset, he will take it out on my mother. George wants to use me to control his business associates. He knows there's no hope that he will ever control Nikolai, so me going away with him will just piss George off.

I stare at my room, feeling lost.

I don't know how long I've been here, trying to sort through everything, but I do know that I'm not prepared when the door opens.

"Are you ready to go, Gabriella?" Nikolai asks.

"What are you doing?"

I don't know if I'm asking him, or myself. I'm so confused about everything right now.

"I think you know the answer to that." I shake my head no, denying him. "Didn't I tell you how I didn't want lies between us?"

"I'm not lying, Mr. Serepova—"

"Nikolai."

"I'm not lying... Nikolai. I don't understand any of this."

He studies me and I do my best not to flinch or withdraw from his heated stare.

"Perhaps it's not lies, perhaps it is confusion then. If so, I shall clear it up. I'm claiming you as my property, Gabriella," he says and I don't think it's my imagination that his voice seems to get deeper and his accent thickens. It sends chills over my body.

"I'm not property. I'm a woman, not a car," I mutter, annoyed despite being intimidated by the unwavering surety in his tone.

"Trust me, Gabriella, I am completely aware of that fact."

"You can't own people, Nikolai."

"In my world, you can," he responds and he says it so matter-of-factly that I really don't know how to respond. "What are your objections about going to Greece with me, Gabriella?" he asks. I get the distinct impression he's annoyed with me, but trying his best to push that aside and for some reason it makes me want to smile. Maybe because in *my* world, men don't hide the fact they're angry and they don't try to spare your feelings. I get the distinct impression Nikolai is doing both and that manages to make me relax with him as nothing else could.

"We don't know each other; more importantly, *I* don't know *you*. You want me to go to another country with you and we've barely spoken," I tell him, deciding to give him complete honesty.

"Isn't that what people do on trips together? Get to know each other?"

I frown, my forehead curling at his logic, because he's kind of right.

"So, we're just going on this trip to get to know one another?"

"Exactly."

"Does this also mean in the biblical sense?"

Now he's the one frowning.

"I'm afraid, I'm not sure I understand," he says proving that he's not technically from America.

"Will we be sleeping together?"

"I want you in my bed, Gabriella."

"I'm not having sex with a man I don't know, Nikolai," I respond and my tension eases even more when he doesn't snap at me. In fact, he smiles. It's a beautiful smile and I'm momentarily hypnotized by it.

"So sex is off the table, but you will share my bed?"

There's something dancing in those eyes of his and I have a feeling I'm walking exactly where he's leading me. It's just that if he keeps smiling like that, I can't think of a single reason why that's not a good thing.

"With my clothes on," I hedge, and for some reason I'm smiling too.

"Deal," he responds and he says it quickly and way too easy. "Now, are you taking anything with you, or are we just going to buy you all new when we get there?"

"That's an option?" I ask, and I know my eyes go wide.

His grin deepens.

"I'll buy you anything you ask for. It will be my pleasure to take you shopping, Gabriella," he says reaching out his hand to me.

I look at it, look at him, and then back to his hand.

"I can ask for a lot of things..."

"I can afford it," he responds, still smiling. He really has no idea what he's about to get into.

"No strings attached right? Sex is still off the table?"

"How about we keep it on the table—"

"I knew it. I think you should—"

"*But*," he starts, interrupting me. "You have to be the one to ask for it."

"You're saying no sex unless I ask for it?" I question in disbelief.

"That's what I'm saying."

"That's not going to happen."

"I think it will."

"I think you're wrong."

"We'll never know if we don't leave. Are you ready?" he says, apparently tired of our back and forth. Which is kind of sad, because I happen to like it a lot.

Nikolai challenges me in ways I've never experienced before. I look at his hand again and then slowly reach out and put mine into it. As his fingers curl around mine, warm tingles spread through my whole body. Those same tingles only increase when Nikolai pulls me in closer to him and puts his hand on my back.

I'm starting to think I'm the one who doesn't know what she's getting herself into.

6

NIKOLAI

I should be working. I have the folder concerning my next business takeover in front of me and I really need to go over the details before my board of directors conference tomorrow. Instead, I find myself looking at Gabriella. It's not that she's beautiful, although she is definitely enchanting. It's not that she is smart and funny, although she's all of those things, too. What I'm discovering and enjoying the most is that she's... *real*.

There's not one fake thing about Gabriella. She talks with the stewardess just like she talks with me. She's genuine. She laughs, she's thoughtful, and she's so damn refreshing that the air even feels cleaner having her close by. She's on my private plane and she's barely batted an eye at any of it, although I guess she's used to riches. George may be broke now, but he had money once and he definitely tries his best to keep up appearances.

Instead, she's been talking with the stewardess about couponing of all things. Apparently, Gabriella once *scored a haul* when she got two hundred dollars of free shampoo, laundry detergent, and fabric softener for three dollars, all by using coupons. The stewardess who has been with me for over a year and rarely speaks other than to ask me if I need anything, immediately became animated. They spent half an hour talking about where to find the best deals. When I couldn't resist asking them what one did with two-hundred dollars' worth of shampoo, they stopped talking, stared at me for barely a moment, then Gabriella gave me a one-word reply.

"Shampoo."

Which, I guess, *did* answer me in a way.

They immediately began talking again and I couldn't help but listen, even when I should have been working.

Now, Gabriella is quiet, but that's because the stewardess left and she's now painting her toenails. I should complain about the Italian leather seats not looking good with her pink toenail polish. Instead, I'd rather replace all the seats on this damn plane as long as she doesn't leave.

I've been obsessed with Gabriella for a while, but after just this limited time with her I know that I will never give her up. I just need to make sure she wants to stay.

"You're staring at me again, Mr. Serepova."

"I told you to call me Nikolai."

"I don't like that name, it doesn't suit you," she argues.

"It's my name."

"So, is Mr. Serepova."

"Gabby—"

"Gabby?"

She stops mid-stroke on painting her toenails to look at me.

"Who said you could call me Gabby?"

"You told Charlotte to call you that," I remind her.

"Charlotte?"

"The stewardess."

"Oh. Well, that's different. She's a friend."

"I want to be your friend, Gabby."

"No you don't. You just want in my pants, Niko."

"Niko?" I laugh, because I don't think there's been one other person in my life that has dared shorten my name like that. I find I like it with Gabriella.

"Unless you'll let me call you Mr. Serepova, without bitching," she suggests.

"That'd be a no."

"Then, Niko it is."

"Then, I'll be calling you Gabby. And, for the record, I do want to be your friend. And I don't want in your pants."

"You don't?" she asks, disbelief so thick in her voice that I have to struggle to keep from laughing.

"I want you out of them," I qualify and Gabby surprises me by throwing her head back and laughing out loud. I just sit there and watch her, and I do it knowing that I've never seen anyone more beautiful in my life.

And I'm pretty sure I never will.

7

GABRIELLA

I like him.

That wasn't supposed to happen. I knew I was attracted to him, but I could have kept that under control, but I like him. I expected cold, aloof, someone that was similar to my stepfather. If life has taught me anything, it's the fact that money changes a person's character. The ones I've met with it, haven't been good people. I expected Nikolai to be much like that.

But he's not.

He's got a dry sense of humor, he's good to the people who works for him, he's attentive, and... *I like him.*

Earlier, he noticed I was shivering. He immediately got up and grabbed a throw off of the bed and brought it back to my seat, covering me with it. He did all of that without a word and as he got back in his chair, he did the strangest thing.

He grabbed my hand and pulled it to his leg. That's it, nothing else, but he wanted my hand on his leg. He wanted me touching him. I'm still processing that and I'm not sure what to do with it. It makes me feel funny inside, but in good ways.

"What?" I ask, jarred, because while I was thinking back on

the day, I had my eyes closed. I wasn't prepared for Nikolai to pick me up.

"It's late, you're dozing off. I'm going to put you in bed. We'll be in Greece when you wake up."

"Oh," I whisper, because I don't know what else to say. My brain isn't exactly working, because instead of arguing with the fact that Nikolai is carrying me to bed, I'm stuck on the thought that I don't think any man has ever carried me anywhere. I'm also pretty sure no one has covered me up when I was cold either— not even when I was a child. So of course, I do the only thing a girl can do. I relax, lay my head on his shoulder and just enjoy.

He lays me down on the bed and I snuggle into the pillow. I close my eyes, but still peek out of them to watch him. I'm feeling warm, happy and even hopeful.

Until he starts to take off his shirt.

"Wait. What are you doing?" I ask, not even bothering to hide the panic in my voice.

"Getting undressed for bed," he says and the bedroom light is out, but the door is open to the main part of the plane and the light from in there glows around him like a halo, showing off his body, his deep tan and that damn smile that makes my insides quiver.

"You said we'd keep clothes on," I remind him, sitting up in bed and clutching the sheets against my breast, even if I am fully dressed.

"I said *you* could keep your clothes on, Gabby, and you can."

"I... but... I can't sleep next to you if you're naked, Niko."

"Why?" he asks, his face clearly showing he doesn't under-stand something that should be simple.

"We're strangers!"

"You're very cute, Gabriella," he murmurs, shaking his head.

He undoes his pants while he is talking though. I cry out— like the scared virgin I am—when I discover the Niko goes commando. I pull the sheets up to my face then, hiding my eyes, as if that is going to shield me. The sound of his laughter echoes around me and I tell myself the reason I peek is to catch his face as he's smiling, and not to get another look at his cock. I'm likely lying to myself, but it won't be the first time.

"I see you checking me out, Princess," he says, calling me on my shit.

"I'll just sleep on the sofa out front," I mutter, moving to slide off the bed.

Nikolai grabs my wrist and refuses to let me go.

"That wasn't the deal, Gabriella. You agreed to lie in bed with me and I want that very thing."

"But, Niko, you're naked."

"Have you never been in bed with a naked man before?"

"I'm not sure that's the kind of question you should ask someone you barely know."

"I know you, Gabriella. I want to know you better, but make no mistake, I *do* know you."

He says it in such a way that I don't want to doubt him, but I really can't help it. How would he know me? There's no way. Our paths have crossed occasionally at George's dinner parties or charity events, but other than the occasional acknowledgment with a 'hello,' we haven't talked. Yes, I know he watched me and part of me thrilled in that knowledge, even if it also terrified me. Still, none of that could be classified as *knowing* me.

"Nikolai—"

"Niko. I like it when you call me that. No one has before. I like that name from your lips, Princess."

"I hate that you call me princess. It makes me sound entitled, or like a pet and I'm not a dog, Niko."

"Agreed, you are more like a kitten with claws, Gabby," he says, settling under the covers. I slowly slide back down to rest my head on the pillow, turning to face him so that we can talk. I try to sort through what I want to say to him.

"Whatever," I respond, but I'm smiling because I like that he called me a kitten. I sigh out loud, because if I'm going to be honest, I like everything about Nikolai.

"And I call you princess because you are regal, Gabriella. Regal, beautiful and you have a way of drawing every eye in the room to you."

"Niko..."

"And to a man like me, who has had very little beauty in his life, I don't think you understand how profound that is. It is refreshing, a simple miracle perhaps, but still a miracle."

"I doubt that. You have beauty all around you, Niko. You have the world at your feet," I remind him.

He reaches out, tucking a piece of my hair behind my ear.

"I have things all around me, Gabby," he says, his voice whisper soft. "That doesn't mean to me they have value. There's more warmth and sweetness in your laugh than I've known most of my life. You, beautiful Gabriella have value."

He says the word value like it's a breath of emotion so deep that it can only be given out a little at a time and with each syllable his lips get closer to mine. I should argue, pull away, tell him that I'm not his, but I don't want to do any of that. I want him to kiss me. I want to mean something to him and I don't want to fight it.

It's as if everything happens in slow motion, until finally his lips are on mine, and our tongues are slowly wrapping around each other. Our kiss is unlike anything I've ever experienced, it's sweet, sexy, heated, but it also feels special. His hand is on my neck, his thumb pressing against my jawline, as he tilts my head so he can claim better access. I lose myself in the kiss, closing my eyes and letting him lead me.

When we break apart, my hands are somehow resting one on

his side and the other on the back of his neck. My leg is thrown over his hip and he has his hand against it, holding it there. My heart is rapidly thumping against my chest. I lick my lips, because I can still taste him there.

"You really know how to kiss," I finally tell him, when I find my voice again.

I keep staring into his dark eyes, unable to pull away and unwilling to move in general. Especially when Niko's lips spread into a deep smile and he freely laughs, his face softening in humor and the sound causing so much joy to rise inside of me that I can't breathe.

It's then I decide that I'll be anything Niko wants...

As long as I get to stay with him.

8

NIKOLAI

"Wake up sleepy head," I murmur against Gabby's ear, breathing in the sweet scent of her. She smells like candy and I definitely want to eat her up. Lying in bed with her through the night was a mixture of pleasure and torture. I loved every minute of it. I wanted more, but I wasn't about to pressure her. I've been too careful up until this point. I'm not about to ruin it now.

"Niko?" she mumbles, her voice still thick with sleep.

Her eyes open, confused, cloudy and *beautiful*. I've always thought she was beautiful. From the moment she first caught my eye, I wanted her. I'd see her at some boring business dinner and I'd lose all train of thought. That doesn't happen to a man like me. I didn't get where I am today by letting a woman distract me. Then again, until Gabriella, women held no lasting interest for me.

Gabriella has long dark hair that makes a man want to wrap his fingers in it, she's got chocolate eyes that I'm sure hold the key to the secrets of the world—at least for me. Her golden skin is sun-kissed, but also completely natural and when she laughs, I swear to God, it sounds like bells.

Yes, I definitely knew I wanted her from the beginning and I bided my time until I could make that a reality. Now that I've actually spent time with her, I know there's no way I'm going to let her go. I'm keeping her.

"Wake up, Princess. It's time to leave."

"Leave? We're in the air," she mumbles, pulling the covers back up over her head.

"We landed an hour ago," I laugh, catching the blanket before she can disappear completely.

"We did?"

"Yeah, we did. So get moving. I want to show you my home."

"I'm hungry," she mumbles.

"What would you like to eat?"

"Fruit?" she asks, and she sounds so hopeful over something as simple as fruit that I shake my head.

"Get ready, there's a place on the beach that has a fruit salad with Kopanisti and—"

"*Copantsty?*"

"Kopanisti. It's a cheese. Get dressed, Gabby. You will see."

"If you leave, I'll get dressed, but I should warn you, Niko."

"Warn me about what?"

"I eat nothing that I can't pronounce."

"I'll help you broaden your horizons, Gabby," I assure her. She shakes her head no, but she's smiling and it's an adorable look with her hair all mussed up around her face.

"Leave, so I can get dressed."

"I could stay here, and you could get dressed in front of me."

"Not going to happen," she says, laughing.

"Can't blame a man for trying," I respond with a wink, walking away, and for the first time in a long time I'm excited for the day ahead.

9

GABRIELLA

"I can't believe you live here," I tell him again. It feels like I've said that a million times, but it's true. This place is as close to paradise as I've ever seen. The waters are a deep turquoise, and the sand even feels different from what I'm used to. Niko's house is square in shape and made out of stone that is painted white.

It looks ancient from the outside, but the inside is so modern it is unlike anything I've been in. The house itself is all one level but it's massive. Room after room feels bigger than anything I've ever been inside of, including a large room that has an all glass wall which opens with a remote control and connects to the outdoor patio and swimming pool. I don't know why you need a pool, because Niko's house is right on the ocean, but it would seem sad without the gorgeous pool, which is almost big enough to be a small lake and is complete with its own fountain.

"As many times as you've mumbled that today, I'm going to guess that you like it," Niko laughs.

"It's beautiful. I've never been to Greece. Everything I've seen is beautiful. Can we sightsee before we go back tomorrow?"

"We're not going back tomorrow, Gabby."

"I mean, I know you must be busy, but I'd just like to see... *What* did you say?"

"We're not going back to the states tomorrow," he repeats, sounding completely casual, like he's not completely rocking my world.

"But you said just overnight and technically it will be two nights, though I didn't really count the one on the plane and if you want to get technical the flight back could make it three and—"

"We're not going back in three days either, Princess."

I swallow... *hard*. Suddenly my throat feels as if it is full of sand.

"Um... Niko... *When* are we going back?"

"I'm not sure. In a couple of months perhaps."

"A couple of..."

I had to have misheard him. There's no way that he's planning on keeping me on an island in Greece for months...

"Niko, I can't stay here for months! I have obligations back home. I'm in school, I have a life!" I know I'm yelling and I know that he can hear the panic in my voice, but I can't help it.

"You have nothing of consequence there. Your life is here with me now."

"Nothing of... *consequence?*"

"Exactly. Now where would you like to go this afternoon?"

"I'm going home. You can go to hell," I huff, pushing my seat back from the table out on the patio.

I can't believe I thought Nikolai Serepova was a good man. He's clinically insane and delusional. That's what he is, not a nice guy at all! I stomp back into the house where I left my shoes and clothes, still wearing the bathing suit and sarong that magically appeared on the bed when we got here. I was so stupid that I didn't even ask who they belonged to, I was just happy that they fit.

I'm an idiot.

"Gabriella, where do you think you're going?" Niko asks, his hand wrapping around my upper arm and turning me around to face him.

He's so handsome. It would be easier to realize he was a stark-raving lunatic if he was ugly.

"Who's bathing suit is this?" I growl. That wasn't what I meant to ask, but now that it's out there, I really want to know.

"What?" he asks, and it doesn't take a brain surgeon to realize he's shocked at my question. I guess no other woman has bothered to call him on being a player.

"Never mind," I huff, not truly wanting to know. For some reason, the thought of Niko with another woman is almost... *painful.*

I try to pull away from him again, but he doesn't let me. In fact, he puts his other hand out and captures me, forcing me to look at him.

"The bathing suit is for you, Gabby. I bought it for you."

"Don't lie to me, Niko. You might think I'm stupid, but I'm not."

"Trust me, I do not think you are stupid, you keep me on my toes in ways no other person has ever been able to."

"Then, you should realize that I'm not going to buy your story that you bought a bathing suit for me. I just got here, you haven't had time to shop for me and there is no way you know my sizes."

"You wear a large top and a size fourteen pants. The bikini you are wearing is a large."

My heart stops—for several reasons. The first being that no woman wants a man she's interested in to know what size she wears—at least not at this stage of a relationship.

Not that Niko and I are in a relationship, but still...

The other reason is that I have no idea how Niko would even begin to guess my size.

"I... I don't understand. Are you saying that you truly did buy this bathing suit for me?"

"I did. I bought it and several others, which you will find in your closet."

"In my... closet..."

"Along with several outfits and lingerie. You'll need more of course, but I just picked out a few things I knew would look good on you. I figured you'd want to shop for the rest."

"I'll need more..." I murmur, my brain slowly catching up with everything he just said.

"I know, that's why I offered to take you shopping."

"I... Niko, when did you pick out clothes for me? We just really spoke to each other for the first time at the party."

"We've spoken before," he corrects me.

"Not much! Just in passing. How did you find time to shop for a trip when we just got here and you've been with me the whole time?"

"I bought the clothes six months ago, Gabriella."

"Six..."

"That's it, do the math, Princess. I bought everything the day of your birthday. The day you turned twenty-one."

"Why?" I ask, and I can't be sure he can even hear me. My heart is beating so loudly in my chest that it is echoing in my ears and it feels like I'm barely whispering.

"Because I've been biding my time until I could claim you. Now that you're twenty-one, you're mine, Gabby."

Oh... Wow.

10

NIKOLAI

Perhaps I should have found a way to slowly ease Gabriella into the truth...

I'm never letting her go.

When she began talking like she was leaving me tomorrow, I snapped. She's not supposed to want to leave me. She sure as hell is not supposed to want to go back to her fucking family.

"That's crazy," she whispers, shock moving over her features.

"No, it's not."

"Niko... it is," she insists and just like it has since the first time she called me that, my dick throbs in reaction. Maybe it is crazy the way that I want her. It's not going to change things though. She needs to accept her fate.

She's staying with me.

"I'm the kind of man who sees what he wants and takes it, Gabby. I want you."

"But, I... That kind of thing might work in business, but I'm a person, Niko. I have my own life. You can't just take someone and hold them hostage."

"Don't make it sound like I'm chaining you up and keeping you against your will, Gabby."

"But you are! I'm in Greece, on an island! We took a boat out here. Will you let the boat take me back into town?"

"Of course."

"I... oh. Okay then," she says. "I'll just go change—"

"We can go back into town and I'll take you shopping. While we are there I can show you—"

"The airport. You can show me the airport," she insists.

"You're not leaving, Gabriella."

"So, you are holding me against my will."

"If you want to twist things around, so be it."

"Twist things around?" she gasps, but I don't let her finish. This needs to be crystal clear.

"Don't act like you don't want to be here, Gabby. Lie to me if you want, but don't lie to yourself. You're as attracted to me as I am to you. You want to be with me, even if you refuse to admit it."

"I wanted to go out on a *date* with you," she corrects me, but all that does is makes me smile.

"Going to Greece with a man at Christmas and agreeing to share his bed isn't a date, Princess."

"I figured it was in your crazy world! And stop making it sound like we're going to sleep together."

"But, we are."

"No, we are—"

Before she can get the lie out of her mouth, I pull her to me and kiss her, holding nothing back because the time for playing with her is over. She needs to embrace this attraction between us, because she's not getting away from me.

The kiss starts off harsh, her frustration and my anger at her denials fuse together and clash as I thrust my tongue into her mouth, conquering and taking what I want. She resists me, or at least tries, managing to pull away enough that our lips break apart. When I dive back in she captures my lip and bites it. She doesn't realize it, but I like that she's a little hellcat. I like that she has fire. I can't wait until I get her in my bed because I know she'll show me enough fire there to burn me alive.

The coppery taste of blood slides into the corner of my mouth. She breathes out deeply and maybe she tries to hide it, but I can tell she's aroused. Her breathing is ragged, her face flushed, she's holding onto me with one hand, her nails biting into my skin, and as my gaze takes in every inch of her, I can see her nipples, hard and pushing against the slick material of her bikini.

"Will you stop kissing me like that," she mutters trying to sound annoyed, but her voice is quieter, and I can hear the arousal in it.

"You don't want me to." I use my thumb to wipe the drop of blood I feel against the corner of my lip.

I do love passion, especially in Gabriella.

"I most certainly do," she responds, sounding huffy as hell.

My hand wraps in her hair, as I use the hold to pull her back to me. She hisses from the sting of pain, but I don't soften my hold. She's going to admit to this pull between us. She's going to admit that she belongs to me.

"If you can tell me that you aren't turned on right now, Gabriella, I will fly you back to Georgia tonight."

"I'm not turned on," she whispers the lie defiantly. My brow furrows in silent rebuttal at her tenacity, as I wait for her to tell me the truth. "I'm not!" she insists.

I move one of my hands down her hip, over her thighs, all while I keep my eyes locked on hers.

"We'll see," I promise her, my voice quiet, but full of the hunger that I've held a tight leash on since knowing that I was going to claim her.

"What..." Gabriella's voice comes out as little more as a

squeak. She quickly takes a breath and tries again. "What are you doing?"

"You don't expect me to let you go without proof that you don't want me, do you, Princess?"

"You have proof. I just told you," she responds, her voice wavering, her eyes dilating so much that the deep brown in them seems to heat and dance for me. A man could lose himself in those eyes.

"I'm afraid I'm going to need more proof than that, Gabby," I reply.

"Niko." She's all but moaning, her voice raspy as the tips of my finger slide against the fabric of her bikini.

"That's it, Gabby. Say my name. Say the name of the man who is going to possess every inch of you."

"I can't—"

My fingers slide under the band of her bikini pushing against the tender skin of her inner thigh. I can feel the heat coming off of her. The skin is damp and as I breathe in deep, I swear I can smell her arousal in the air. Her breath is coming out in pants now. Little puffs of air that are loud, delectable exhales. What will she sound like when I'm sliding inside of her? Will her breath come out even harder as I'm tunneling in and out of her body, fucking her so hard that she will be able to feel me for days? The tips of my fingers slide against the lips of her pussy, I moan when I find them bare.

Bare and wet.

"Are you going to deny that you want me now, Gabriella?" I groan, my finger edging closer to her entrance.

"I want you, Niko," she responds, a tremor of need moving through her body, snapping what little control I have left.

"That's my Princess," I rasp. I take her mouth, while my fingers slide between her lips and seek out her clit.

Finally... she's mine.

11

GABRIELLA

Maybe I'm weak. Maybe I should try to deny this attraction with Niko. I'm tired of fighting it, however. I want him. I've wanted him from the moment I first saw him and I was only nineteen. It's one of the reasons I always tried to stay far away from him. I called it self-preservation. The truth is, I knew I wanted him, but I knew he wasn't for me. Yet, here he is kissing me, his hand...

Oh God, his hand.

His fingers are pressing against my entrance, the tips pushing in and my knees instantly go weak. I moan his name as I feel him move to my clit, sliding over the point where I need him the most right now. His mouth swallows the sound, devouring, eating at my lips and I am just as desperate for him. He tastes earthy, musky and forbidden. I know I shouldn't give in, but I can't stop myself.

The kiss is beautiful. *Beautiful and brutal.* It's as if we're waging war on one another, but it's so good that there's no way to stop it.

"So fucking wet and hot. You're going to burn me alive. Aren't you, Princess?" Niko groans against my neck. The sound is so raw that it makes me quiver with need almost as much as the way his fingers are sliding against my throbbing clit.

"Stop talking," I demand, wanting more of his mouth, wanting more of him. He laughs, but the sound is muffled as I find his mouth and initiate our kiss again, my tongue pushing into his mouth, needing more.

His hand plunges back into my hair, as he takes over the kiss and I don't care. I don't care about anything as long as he keeps kissing me and his other hand—the one with the magic fingers—keeps moving. He positions my head where he wants me, he savages my mouth in a way that I know my lips will be bruised and I love it.

I. Love. It.

As long as he doesn't stop, he can do anything he wants. He uses his hold on my hair to pull my head back. I cry out, but not from the pain. It's because I'm not ready for him to stop kissing me. His kisses are addicting and I never want them to end.

"Has anyone been inside this sweet little cunt, Gabriella?"

His voice is graveled, as if he smokes three packs of cigarettes a day. His words filthy and growled into my ear, thrust through me and I feel my excitement pool against his fingers. There's so much that I'm almost afraid I'm coming now. I want to, but I also want it to last longer. I *need* it to last longer. I whimper when I fight against his hold, hoping to find his mouth again, but he doesn't let me move.

"Answer me, Princess. Has another man been inside of you?" he orders.

"No," I admit. "No one."

He rewards me by kissing my neck, his tongue following an imaginary path to my ear as he sucks the lobe into his mouth. "Have they touched you like I'm touching you?" he whispers, his voice feeling like a touch.

"No." I'm mindless, answering anything he wants, giving him

anything he wants as long as he doesn't stop. "I've never wanted anyone," I add, giving him my guilty little secret. It's always been so easy playing the role that George, my stepfather, gave me. Because I've never had one person in my life who made me come alive as a woman. Just Niko.

And I knew.

I knew all along, from the first moment I saw him that I was his. The feeling was so huge that it scared me and I tried to deny it. I tried, until Niko refused to let me.

"You want me, Gabriella. Admit it. You belong to me. You are mine." His hand moves from my hair to my neck. He turns me so that I'm against a wall and he's pushing against my front. The entire time his fingers are still sliding against my wet clit, teasing it lightly and bringing me closer to my climax, but never letting me get completely there.

"Niko, please." I know I'm begging and I don't care. I'll beg as long as he stops denying me.

His fingers switch directions and I moan from the ache they create and before I can catch my breath he manages to somehow pinch my clit. My body jerks in reaction, my head falling back against the wall

"Answer me, Gabriella," he orders, the sternness in his voice not allowing for argument. "Who do you belong to? Who were you *made* for my, Milen'kiy."

I know he's speaking Russian. I have no idea what he's saying, but the word thrills me just the same.

"You," I whisper, letting the final wall tumble down between us. "I belong to you, Niko."

"Finally," he breathes out triumphantly. "Come for me, Princess. Come on my hand and show me how much you want me and when you're done, I'm going to carry you into our bedroom and fuck you hard and raw."

His words should scare me, but they don't. I love them. He

grinds his fingers against me and I thrust into them, following his lead. I'm so close, I know I'm going to explode. I'm almost there when...

"Damn, brother. Have we come at the wrong time?"

Niko's hand stops, my body goes solid. My eyes open, I turn to look over Niko's shoulder, as I hold onto his body. I see three men standing behind us, staring straight at me... My head drops down onto Niko as embarrassment floods me. I hear him curse under his breath as my body mourns the loss of his fingers.

12

NIKOLAI

My brothers always have had horrible timing, but I think this is one of the worst times I can ever remember. I can hear the laughter in Victor's voice. I would like nothing more than to slam my fist into his face. I'm frustrated enough to do that very thing. I know, however, that it would just make all three of them worse. I don't have many things in this world that I'm connected to, but my brothers are definitely one.

Victor, Mikal, and Andrey.

Victor is the oldest, then me, followed closely by Mikal and Andrey—who are twins. I pull my hand regretfully from beneath Gabriella's bikini. I lean out just enough so that I can look into her eyes. Her face is flushed, the color deepening in her cheeks, then moving down her neck and across her chest. I hate that she still has her bikini on, I would like to see her whole body flushed with hunger. Although, I know that right now part of her coloring is because of embarrassment. I look deeply into her eyes, our gazes lock as I slowly bring my fingers between us.

"Niko," Gabriella gasps. Even though, she's embarrassed and wants to leave, I can still hear the hunger in her voice.

"It's okay, Milen'kiy," I respond softly, taking my free hand and brushing her hair and cupping the side of her neck. "Out!" I order my brothers.

"But, Nikolai, we are so enjoying the show," Victor laughs.

"Get out, I won't tell you again."

My brothers all laugh, but at least they are walking away. I wait until they're completely out of the room, then I demand Gabriella's attention.

"Look at me, Gabby." She slowly brings her face back up, her gaze locked with mine. "You are beautiful, my love."

Once I'm sure that I have her attention, I put my fingers into my mouth licking them clean, and letting her watch.

"Oh, God," she whimpers, a fine shiver running through her body. "Niko, who are those people?"

"I'm sorry, Gabby. Those are my brothers and as you can tell, they have very bad timing."

"Oh, God... They saw us. They saw *me*."

"They saw nothing. What we just shared is for us and us alone. Trust me, Gabby, they might have been giving me a hard time just then, but they will not say anything else to you."

"But what if—"

"There are no ifs. It will be fine, you will see. How about you go upstairs to your room and get ready for dinner. You can try out one of the new dresses I bought you."

"But, they, I mean..."

"It's all going to be fine, Princess. You just get ready for dinner, I'll handle my brothers."

She walks away, muttering under her breath. "I didn't even know you had brothers."

"Soon, Milen'kiy. Soon, you will know everything and trust in what we are."

"What are we?" she asks so quietly that I have to strain to hear her.

"Forever, Gabriella. We are forever."

She takes in my words, her face softening, her eyes warming and the stress I saw there moments earlier disappears.

"What's your favorite color Niko?"

"Red," I respond, not sure why she asked, but willing to tell her anything.

"Is there a red dress in my closet?"

I smile when I see her grinning at me, mischief on her face.

"There is, actually. There are two red ones."

"Do you have a preference?"

I smile, because I know what she has in mind now and the satisfaction I feel is hard to explain. She wants to please me. I don't even have to think to answer her.

"The longest one. I'd rather not have to kill my brothers for staring at your legs all night," I respond, only half joking.

Gabby surprises me then. She throws her head back, laughing. The sound is enchanting, real, and the best thing I've ever heard. I've never been a lighthearted man, but having Gabby's laughter the last two days makes me feel as if I am.

"I'll see what I can do," she murmurs, still laughing as she goes up the stairs. I watch her until she disappears out of sight. Then, I head to the restroom to wash my hands. My brothers will have to wait. I don't want them to get one whiff of Gabby's arousal. That's mine and mine alone.

13

GABRIELLA

I fall back on the bed with a huge exhale of air. My mind is going a million miles a minute as I relive what just happened. I wasn't expecting that. I don't know what I was expecting, but it wasn't *that*. Nikolai wants me. I mean, that's not a huge surprise, but I think he wants to *keep* me.

And, I kind of want him to.

I've never felt like this before. My heart is still racing in my chest and my body is on fire. As great as it is, though, I need to get back to Georgia. I don't have a choice. Niko doesn't understand about my stepfather, but I'll have to tell him. I'm afraid if I don't go back, he'll make my mother pay for it. I'm not close with my mother, but I don't want to be the reason that he hits her.

My stepfather is controlling with an edge of violence that intimidates me. I'd leave completely and never look back if not for my mother. She hasn't been the greatest parent, but she's still my mom and she's provided for me, kept a roof over my head.

Thinking about it depresses me, so I get up and take a shower. I do my best not to relive what happened with me and Niko while in the shower. I was left hanging. I didn't get to come, but without Niko, finishing myself off has no appeal. In the past I've masturbated, and at the time I thought it felt good. Niko definitely blew that misconception out of the water.

I wrap a towel around my body and then decide to check out this closet that Niko told me had clothes he bought for me. When I open it, I'm pretty sure I stop breathing. Inside there are dresses, the likes I've never seen and since George likes to make sure his friends think he has money—while using me to distract some of the men, he gets me the latest designer gowns. His are definitely on the risqué side, too which are different from the ones I'm looking at now. I've never seen dresses as beautiful as the ones in this closet. They're definitely sexy, but they're more refined, meant to tease instead of going for the gusto all at once. There are two red dresses, just like Niko said, but there are also at least six others and the colors are all colors that I tend to gravitate toward —black, green, and silver. A strange, fluttery sensation moves through me.

Niko said he knew me. He said he'd been planning this since my birthday. I didn't truly believe him, but can it be a coincidence that these dresses are styles I'd choose? Colors—with the exception of the red—that I'd buy myself? There are more bikinis and a couple of one-piece bathing suits, some capris and pants with coordinating shirts and every one of the items have the tags hanging on them, proving no one else has ever worn them.

There is now not one single doubt in my mind that Niko was telling the truth. He went shopping specifically for me.

The closet is huge and when I open the second door, that fluttering sensation gets stronger. Niko's clothes are there, and seeing them hanging so close to clothes meant for me affects me in ways that I can't totally describe. Looking at our clothes together like that doesn't feel wrong either.

It feels unbelievably right.

What am I going to do about Niko? How am I going to get in charge of this situation again?

I walk back out into the main bedroom and there's a wall with a large built in wardrobe, in an ivory color. I think I'm shaking as I reach out and pull on one of the drawers.

Lingerie. The sexiest, most delicate lingerie I've ever seen, but all of it is in one color. There's differing shades of it, but it's still one certain color.

Red.

There are still tags on them too, but there's no doubt whatsoever that while the other clothes Niko might have bought for me, the silky lace items he wants me to wear to bed?

They are definitely all for him.

All of this leads me to ask one question again and again.

What *am* I going to do about, Niko?

14

NIKOLAI

"He looks a tad pissed, don't you think, Mikal? Andrey laughs.

"I'd bet on a different emotion. You seem to have your flag pole standing at attention, Nikolai," Victor says with a smirk, taking a drink of my good vodka.

I kick his feet off of the stool in front of his chair and sit down, staring at my brothers. I was probably an asshole, but I made my brothers wait close to an hour before I joined them. Instead, I went to my office and made reservations for all of us for dinner tonight. I wanted them to meet Gabriella, but I also wanted to make sure that we went some place nice to show her off. I wanted to dance with her, too. I always want Gabriella in my arms and dancing is the easiest way to make that happen in public—especially if my brothers make her uneasy, which they just might do unless I stop it. Which is why I've decided to join them now. They need to understand just how important Gabriella is to me. I won't put up with them harassing her just to get to me.

"What are you assholes doing here unannounced?"

"It's Christmas. Do we need any other reason?" Mikal asks.

"Greece is a long way from the U.S. or Russia," I point out.

"But it is the time of year that families should be together," Andrey says and I know that's bullshit. We rarely get together as a family and none of us pay any attention to holidays. Until having Gabby in my life, I've never thought much about taking time to enjoy Christmas. Gabby makes me want to take time for a lot of things.

"I'm waiting."

"We haven't spoken in months it seems, Nikolai," Victor says and I give him my attention, because of the three of my brothers he is definitely the more serious. The twins are pranksters and I'm not sure they have taken anything serious in their life.

"This is not unusual," I point out and it's not. My brothers and I are close in our own way, but we didn't grow up in a family that was close and thoughtful. We are there for one another when we need to be, but it is not unusual to go three or four months without a word from any of us. Self-sufficient is a way of life in the Serepova household. Both our parents were career military and were not cut out to be parents. I'm not even sure how they had children, considering they hate one another in the first place.

"True, but we always keep one another up to date with what is going on in life," Mikal responds.

"So?"

"So, imagine our surprise when the glad-rags in America begin flashing our brother's picture everywhere with this pretty young girl and announcing their engagement."

"Shit," I mumble when Andrey announces that little tidbit.

"You don't trust women, Nikolai and you definitely don't do things on the spur of the moment, you're a planner—as we all are. So tell me, dear brother, what is actually going on here?" Victor asks, and he's definitely all business now. I stand up, walking to look out over the pool. Not because I'm upset with the announcement about my personal life. I knew after my talk with Gabriella's stepfather that the rat would waste no time. Still, I would have liked to secure her acceptance of our marriage before she found out about it. Which means I need to make my brothers promise not to let the cat out of the bag just yet.

"Nikolai?" Mikal prompts me and I can hear a small amount of worry in his voice. I turn to face him, face all of them.

"She is the one," I tell them, giving them everything in those four words.

"The one?" Victor asks, and he understands immediately.

Then again, why wouldn't he? As boys my brothers and I all discussed never settling when it came to women. We all knew that we wanted that one special woman and if she never appeared we would never get married, never have the type of relationship our parents obviously had.

"She's it for me."

"Damn," Victor whistles.

"You're sure?" Andrey asks, and all signs of joking is gone.

"Never been surer of anything in my life, Andrey."

"Maybe you're mistaken, Nikolai. It has happened so fast."

"Bullshit, Mikal. I have been planning this for over a year."

"Over a year?" Why is it just now happening then?" Victor asks.

"She is young. I didn't want to touch her until she was legal," I shrug.

"Fuck, she's seventeen? I know she looked young from looking at that tight ass, but damn Nikolai."

I walk over to Andrey and use the heel of my palm to slug Andrey on the side of the head.

"She's twenty-one, dumbass. And you keep your eyes off of her ass. I would hate to have to kill my own brother."

"You're positive then. She's the one."

"Yes, and I'm claiming her. I just need your help with one thing."

"Our help with what? I mean if you won't even let me look at her ass, I'm not sure what I can help with concerning her," Andrey says with a smirk, proving that I could hit him twice a day, every day, and he still wouldn't learn a damn thing.

"I don't want you to tell her what you read about the engagement. Gabriella has no idea and I don't want you three throwing a wrench into my dealings with her. I have to approach this carefully with Gabby. She can be a little resistant," I tell them with a smile, thinking that doesn't exactly describe what Gabriella's response will be. She'll most likely give me hell. In the end however, I will get her to agree—even if I have to fuck her senseless to get her agreement. That idea is quite appealing and I kind of hope that's what it takes. She will say yes and that's all that matters.

"Resistant? Does that mean she might make you beg?" Mikal laughs, sounding like he would enjoy that possibility very much.

"Probably." I sigh as I confess that and sit back down, finding I don't even care. Gabriella is everything I ever wanted in a woman and I'm more and more positive of that as I spend time with her.

"Damn, you're in love," Victor says his voice quiet. I look at him. I think of denying it, but there's no point.

"Love seems a tepid word for what I feel for Gabriella. Still, I guess you can call it that if you wish. I just know that she's mine and I am never letting her go."

"We're happy for you, Nikolai," Andrey says and all of my brothers are nodding their heads in agreement.

"Thank you. Does this mean you will do your part and *not* tell, Gabriella?" I ask, leveling my gaze on each of them, daring them not to agree.

"Tell me what?" Gabriella asks.

I look up at her, standing there looking gorgeous in one of the red dresses I picked out for her, and her long hair pulled up on top of her head, making my fingers itch to tear it down. I'm lost for a moment just looking at how breathtaking she is—which is a big mistake because I should have been stuffing my fist in Andrey's mouth so the bastard couldn't talk.

"He doesn't want us to tell you that you're engaged and getting married," Andrey says helpfully to Gabriella.

Shit.

15
_____

GABRIELLA

It's official.

Nikolai and his entire family are insane.

"We're not getting married."

"Are you ready for dinner, Milen'kiy?"

"Nikolai, tell them we're not getting married," I demand.

"We'll discuss it later, Princess. We don't want to be late for our reservation."

He kisses my forehead, taking me into his arms for a small hug and then, with his hand on my back, begins ushering me out of the room. Stubbornly, I refuse to move.

"I'm not going to ignore this, Niko. I'm not going to just forget about it. We are not getting married."

"Would being married to me be so bad, Gabriella?" he asks and I get the impression that I'm offending him. Shit. Maybe I'm even hurting his feelings. I know guys can have egos the size of Texas.

"Niko, we don't know each other."

"I think I've proven how wrong that is, at least on my part. Besides, eventually you will get to know me."

"Eventually I'll get to know you," I mumble under my breath. I'm not really talking to him, I'm just repeating what he said because I can't truly believe it.

"Exactly. Now, let's all head to the restaurant. I made reservations at a traditional Greek restaurant that I think you will enjoy—"

"When do you suppose I'll get to know you, Niko?"

"Gabriella—"

"I mean, you said I would eventually. When do you think that will be?"

"Milen'kiy, we're going to be late for dinner."

"Will it be before our fiftieth wedding anniversary, do you suppose?"

His brothers laugh, but I ignore them. They're as crazy as he is. Niko looks at me, his eyes going soft and he steps so close into me that I suddenly have trouble breathing. His fingers sift through a curled tendril of my hair that I left down, as his hand moves to slide against the side of my neck. He tilts my head back to look at him and my heart trips over in my chest at the pleasure I see on his face.

"We will celebrate that fiftieth year, Milen'kiy. That and many more after that. But, I can promise you that you will know everything there is to know about me before our first child is born."

"I... I'm not sure how to respond to that. We're having children together?" I ask, hope and fear warring in my chest.

"Several and soon. I want my child planted inside of you, Gabriella. I want to watch your body change as you nurture the life that the two of us create together. I want to be there as you feed him for the first time," he says, his voice dropping down and the back of his hand brushing against the underswell of my breasts.

I'm lost to everything but Niko at this point. Hypnotized by his words, lost in a world that he seems to be creating in my mind. A world where we are married and having children and blissfully happy. A world that might not be real, but I want it to be so bad that it hurts.

"Niko..."

"You will marry me, Gabriella, so we can have all of those children."

"I..."

"And, we will be together for fifty years and longer. You are my forever, Milen'kiy. I'm not letting you go."

"You scare me," I confess.

"But, you like it," he argues and I do.

"If I tell you that I do, is that going to make you even bossier?" I mumble, my brain officially a blob of goo.

"Gabriella, moya sestra, I do believe it is time we get to know one another."

My head jerks up as one of Niko's brothers comes over and literally pulls me out of Niko's arms, breaking the moment.

"Victor," I hear Niko growl, but Victor ignores him and instead begins talking to me.

"Have you ever been to Greece before? Nikolai prefers it, but myself, I like Russia. The twins, they choose the United States, but we all do try to visit one another from time to time," he says, but I'm barely paying attention. I look over my shoulder at Niko, who doesn't appear happy. His other brothers fall in step beside him as they follow us. I force myself to talk with Victor, wondering how life got so out of hand...

16

NIKOLAI

"You are quiet, Milen'kiy."

"It's been a full day," she says, but she still seems reserved, even with that reply.

I close the door to our bedroom, leaning against it as I watch her. She kicks off her shoes, one at a time and then slowly walks to the dresser, taking off her earrings.

"That doesn't explain why you barely spoke through dinner."

"I spoke, Niko," she says—not looking at me.

"To my brothers, you barely spoke to me." My tone is borderline harsh and my impatience is bleeding through it. I don't like that she's been basically ignoring me the entire night.

"I was being friendly. After all, you tell me that they are going to be my new family."

"They are, but it would be nice if you would try and be friendly with your fiancé."

She doesn't respond. Instead, she walks into the adjoining bath and begins washing her face. I sit on the bed watching her, undoing my cufflinks, kicking off my shoes and taking off my tie.

I'm completely undressed except for my pants and she's yet to come back into the room.

"Gabriella," I warn, when finally she comes back, but instead of talking she continues to ignore me. If that wasn't bad enough, she's wearing one of my t-shirts. It drapes over her body and falls to just above her knee. I'm torn because I love that it is my shirt she wears, but I don't want her to have clothes on in our bed. I also bought her a ton of expensive lingerie to wear.

"I'm going to sleep, Nikolai," she says, turning her back to me and sliding into bed on the other side. I take off the rest of my clothes and then pull the covers over me, as I pull her stiff body back against mine. Even then, she doesn't argue.

"You're going to explain why you ignored me all night and why you are obviously pissed now," I murmur in her ear, keeping her back firmly pressed against my front, my arms around her, locking her to me so she can't escape.

"I'm tired, Nikolai," she says, fighting to get out of my hold.

"Then you can sleep, but after you tell me why you are pissed at me."

She elbows me in the stomach. It's not hard, but enough that I let her go. She flops over on her back and I lean up so I can look at her face and see her while we talk. I need to be able to read her emotions and thankfully Gabriella is unpracticed at hiding those. Everything she feels is apparent on her beautiful face.

"Why? I would think that is pretty well self-explanatory, Niko."

"Humor me."

"How many people do you know find out they're engaged through their future in-laws, Niko?"

"Quite a few actually, Milen'kiy. I am from Russia. Not all, but quite a few marriages, at least in my circle, are arranged."

"Well, they're not here. And quit calling me that! What does it even mean anyway?"

"My darling."

"Oh. It's kind of pretty, but that's not the point."

"What is the point, Gabby."

"The point is, you aren't supposed to tell your brothers we are getting married before you even *ask* me!"

"I didn't tell them."

"I mean, really. I know you are big on just telling me how it's going to be and then... Wait. *You didn't?*"

"No. I didn't mention it at all."

"Then, why did they think we are getting married?"

"We *are* getting married, Gabriella."

"Maybe. How did they know if you didn't mention it, Niko?"

"We are," I insist, my eyes boring into hers. "And they read it."

"Read it?"

"Your stepfather announced our engagement after we left. It's not a big issue, really. Although, I wish he had waited until we returned stateside and were already married. He'll be expecting a huge wedding now, which he will turn into a business matter and I don't want our marriage starting off like that."

"My stepfather... Why would he do that?" she asks and I don't like the panic in her voice.

"Because I told him you were mine now and that neither your mother nor him had any say when it came to you."

"You told him that," she says, her voice sounding different, but I can't quite explain why.

"Yes."

"And why would he agree to that, Niko?"

"Because he had no choice. I know it's hard for you to understand, Gabriella, but some people might think marrying me was a good thing, damn it," I growl, losing my patience.

"I know that, damn it," she yells back. "I just don't understand how everyone seems to know besides me. Also, I know my stepfather and he wouldn't just take this easily. He wanted..."

"Yes, Gabriella, why don't you tell me what your stepfather *wanted*."

"I... I don't want to talk about this," she mutters.

"He was going to marry you off to that fucking Stanford Willoughby who is old enough to be your father."

"Technically you are too, Niko. Although, much younger."

"Gabriella," I warn.

"He couldn't have married me off to Stanford. I wouldn't have allowed it," she says with a sigh. "I only let him have his way with the other shit to protect my mother. I would have never agreed to marry Stanford. He's actually old enough to be my grandfather."

"Why are you protecting your mother, Gabriella?" I ask, my voice softening.

I fall back on the bed and then gather my woman in my arms and bring her over me. I push her hair behind her ear, admiring the delicate shape. Hell, I love everything about her.

"George has a temper..."

"Has he ever hit you, Milen'kiy?"

"Not me," she hedges. "He's never needed to."

"Because you've given in to what he has asked?"

"It's not been that bad, Niko. He likes to use me as a distraction, parade me around—"

"I know what he's been doing, Gabby. What I don't understand is why you agreed? I can tell you hate it. Why didn't you leave? Was it a money issue?"

"You think I care that much about the money?" she asks, and I can see her face color. I can't tell if it's embarrassment or anger, but I think it might be a mixture of both.

"I think the thought of not having money once you're used to it can be frightening."

"You know nothing. I'd be fine without it. I work off campus now. I use as little of my stepfather's money as possible. I have school loans and I worked my ass off for a scholarship. If it wasn't for the travel he demands and those damn parties, I would never touch his money," she insists and I can tell she's completely serious and I hate that I offended her.

"Then why?"

"Because my mother and I might not be close, but I don't want to see her sporting a black eye, or worse, and know that I could have prevented it," she mumbles, avoiding my eyes again.

"I should have had him arrested," I growl,

"You could do that?"

"George is broke, Princess. He's been using the money his clients put up for investing to float his business and pay his bills, while inflating the losses on what money he does invest."

"Oh my God."

"I discovered it a while back, when I was searching for a way to control him."

"Control him?"

"I told you that I saw you and knew you would be mine. There was no way I was going to let him stand between us. Therefore, I needed a way to contain him. I found it."

"George isn't the kind of man to take that lightly Niko. I know him. Why would he willingly announce our engagement?"

"Because I gave him three million reasons why he should accept that he has no control over you now."

"Three million.... You gave my stepfather *three million dollars*?"

"I underpaid him, Milen'kiy."

"I can't breathe."

"Gabriella," I start, but she pulls away, sliding off the top of me. I let her go, but only so I can stretch alongside her and lean over her. I capture her wrists in my hand and push them against the mattress, refusing to let her go anywhere.

"Let me go, Niko."

"Never, I told you, you are mine."

"You're right, I am."

She gives me the words I want, but her voice is cold as she says it. There are tears in her eyes too and God help me, I'd do anything to keep her from crying.

"Gabriella—"

"I mean you paid three million dollars for me. How can I *not* be yours?" she asks, and the tears she's managed to hold at bay start falling and as each one of them drops, it feels like a knife being thrust in my chest.

I have no idea how I'm going to fix this... I just know I have to.

17

GABRIELLA

I can't stand the embarrassment and the pain. Niko basically paid for me. I don't know how to process it, and I don't know how to feel about it. Any woman would be flattered by catching Niko's eye, by having his attention. Still, I don't want to be an item he *purchased*.

And that's exactly how I feel.

"Let me go, Niko," I beg, feeling so much humiliation that I'm almost choking on it.

"I can't. Don't you see, "Milen'kiy?"

"All I can see is that you paid for me and that makes me no better than a whore."

"Bullshit. You're a virgin for Christ's sake. How could you think I thought of you as a whore?"

"Oh, I don't know, Niko. Maybe because you paid for me!"

"I paid your stepfather so he wouldn't be an issue in your life anymore. I did that because of you, Gabriella."

"I know you did it so I—"

"I did it so you wouldn't worry about your parents. I did it because your feelings matter to me. I don't see why this is a bad thing. I told your stepfather he should be glad that I do care about you, because if I didn't, he would be in jail."

"It's still completely mortifying, Niko. Can't you see that?"

"Why? You aren't the imbecile who fleeced his clients."

"You really can't see it? You can't be so crazy that you don't understand that no woman wants to be property a man purchases."

"Milen'kiy, how can you say that? What I did was to protect you. I have wanted you for over a year, if you think for one minute that I give a damn about that money, you are the crazy one."

"Stop, just stop. It was three *million* dollars, Niko!"

"And I would have given twice that, hell three times that, if it meant that in doing so I could shelter you from pain, Gabriella."

I start to reply, but then the gravity of his words hit me. The look on his face, cuts through my embarrassment and anger. It finally registers that Niko believes everything he's saying.

It's finally hitting home that this isn't about a business deal or money with him. It's about me and what he can do to make things better for me.

"It's too much, Nikolai."

"It's not enough, Gabriella. I will do whatever I have to do to make sure you are safe and happy. Money is not my focus. My focus is on you. It has been from the moment I first saw you and it's never going to change."

"You're trying to make me fall in love with you," I whisper.

"You are fucking right I am. I want you tied to me in so many different ways that you never want to break free, Gabby. I won't rest until you are."

"How will I know that you feel the same way about me?" I ask him softly.

"What?"

"If I'm going to be tied to you, Niko. How will I know that you won't tire of me? That you won't one day replace me?"

"My silly, Gabriella. I am obsessed with you. You are all I have thought about from the moment I first laid eyes on you. From the moment I looked at you, all other women ceased to exist. You are everything to me, Princess. You are my woman, my heart, my family, my life. One day soon you will be the mother of my child, my lover, and definitely my wife."

My heart stutters as I look at Nikolai. This is crazy and it's all happening so quickly. Then again, if he's been plotting for over a year, maybe it's not quick at all. All I know, is that it feels right and I want to belong to Niko. I don't want to leave him and the rest ultimately doesn't matter.

"Niko," I whisper and maybe he can sense the change in my voice, because he lets go of my hands. I bring one of them up to hold the side of his face lovingly.

"Yes, Gabby?" he says, his voice husky.

"We could probably make at least one of those come true tonight," I tell him.

"One of those?"

"Yes, maybe two, you never know."

"What are you—"

"Make love to me, Niko. I want to belong to you in every way possible. I want you to belong to me," I tell him, looking him in the face and baring my heart to him. I think that's okay though, because I've never felt safer in my life.

18

NIKOLAI

It's surprising the heavens don't open up and the angels sing when Gabriella tells me to make love to her. It feels like I've waited a million years for those words, even if I haven't.

"Are you sure, Milen'kiy. I don't want you to feel pressured," I offer her, like an idiot.

In response, Gabriella surprises me. She's no shy little virgin with me at all. Instead, she reaches down between us, wraps her hand around my cock and strokes me. Her hand is firm, her movements are almost painfully slow, as my cum gathers on the head of my cock. I need to hurry and take control or this girl will have me coming before her, and that can never happen. I need to be inside of her.

"You wouldn't play with me if you knew how long I've been dying to have you, Gabriella," I warn her, unable to look away from her beautiful face or the softness in her eyes.

"Maybe I like to play with you, Niko. I feel safe with you," she says and fuck...Out of everything she could have said, that means more than anything. I want her to feel safe, I want her to be herself with me. I will do everything in my power to make sure she always feels at ease with me.

I put my hand over hers, together we move my cock so that the tip pushes against the lips of her pussy. Gabriella's eyes dilate, her teeth capturing her bottom lip to stifle the gasp that leaves her, as I slip inside and slide the tip of my cock against her wet pussy.

"You are safe with me, Gabriella. You will always be safe with me."

"I know, Niko."

"I'll take care of you, Milen'kiy," I promise with a growl, letting my hand slide down my shaft and dip between her legs so my fingers can push through her cream. She's so wet, the inside of her thighs are painted with it. The minute she feels my fingers there, her hungry pussy tries to latch onto them. Her muscles clamp down, and I can feel how she immediately begins to spasm. One movement from me, one well-placed twist on her throbbing little clit, and she'd go off like a Roman candle. I'm right there with her and as tempting as it is to let her come, I can't. I want us to come together. I want my cock buried so deep inside of her that I feel everything when she comes for the first time. I want to bathe her womb with my seed and claim her in every way possible.

I use my free hand to comb her hair gently, letting my fingers drift over her face, a face that owns me.

"I don't know any way for this not to hurt, Gabriella. But, I promise you, if you just hold onto me, it will get better," I try to assure her, hoping like hell that I'm telling her the truth.

"I know, Niko. I'm ready. I'm not worried. I want this, I want to belong to you," she tells me, almost shyly. Her hands move over my shoulders and face, much like mine did on her moments before and nothing has ever felt so sweet. I let my cock sink another inch, not breaching her virginity, but letting her get used to me as slowly as possible.

Her pussy enfolds my cock with its wet heat. She starts to tense, and I pet her with my hand, holding still, and waiting. Her fingers are now holding onto my shoulder and I can feel her nails biting into me.

"Shh... I'm going to go slow, Milen'kiy, and you're going to be in control."

"I'm in control?" she asks, her voice sounding confused, but I can still hear her desire.

"Exactly. Press your feet against the mattress, Gabriella," I order her softly. It takes her a minute, but she does and I smile at her reassuringly. "Now, bring your hand back to my cock."

The minute she does, I want to come. It takes more control than I ever thought possible not to blow, especially when she nervously strokes me. "None of that, Milen'kiy. I can't handle it, I'm too close to the edge. When I come, I'm going to be buried as deep into you as I can go. I want you to feel me for days. Every time you walk, I want you to feel my cum drip down your leg and know who you belong to."

"Nikolai... I'm not protected. I don't take anything. Birth control, I mean," she whispers. Her face blushing a deep pink that blooms down her neck and over her pretty rose tipped breasts. "You need to wear...a condom," she whispers.

"I don't want anything between us Gabby. We are having children together, why wait? I don't want to worry about using something. I need it to be my cock you feel inside of you, not latex."

"Are you sure?"

"Completely. We start our lives together from this moment on, Milen'kiy."

It might make me an asshole, but I don't want to back down from this. I want Gabriella pregnant with my child. I want her stomach stretched with my baby. That thought alone makes my cock jerk within her soft hold.

"Okay," she whispers, smiling at me, and I can see happiness there, making me relax. I've waited so long, but finally, Gabriella is mine.

"Now, keep your hand at the base of my cock. You are the one that will control how deep I go. If you don't like it, squeeze and hold me, I won't go any deeper until you're ready."

"Okay," she whispers, licking her lips. I can't resist bending down to kiss her. My tongue slips inside and seeks out hers. I kiss her slowly, refusing to rush, letting her know with that simple kiss how much I care about her.

My cock slips a little deeper inside of her. She's so tight that my whole damn body vibrates with the need to thrust through her virginity and bury myself in her. I'm barely inside of her and her muscles are already claiming my cock and demanding more. I study her face and I know that she loves the feel of this. Hell, she's pulling on my cock, wanting me deeper—just as much as I need to be there. She's so ready that it would be easy to slide home, but I'm stretching her tight little cunt and I know I need to go slow.

"I need more, Niko," she says, practically humming my name.

"Soon, but we need to go slow, I don't want to hurt you. Tell me how you feel."

"I'm so...*full*."

God, she is. I'm stretching the hell out of her. It feels so fucking good that I am not sure how I'll ever leave her.

"I know, Milen'kiy, but does it feel good?"

"Yes, you're inside of me," she says, almost reverently. "We're a part of each other now." She's so innocent and untouched by the world. I don't know how that happened, but I like that she doesn't have walls. I love that I don't have to guess what she's thinking.

She innocently thinks this is farther along than it is. The truth is that I'm barely inside of her. If I don't take over now, this will end before I've claimed her. Even now, my balls are tight and ready for release.

I hold my hands on her hips and pull her gently, holding her still the moment I feel my cock pushing against thin veil of her virginity. I stop and close my eyes trying to gain self-control.

"Niko?" she questions, jerking in my hold.

"Hold your tits out for me, Milen'kiy. Hold them out for my mouth," I encourage her. I don't really need that, but getting her to do that will get her to let go of my cock. I need the freedom to thrust all the way inside of her. I'm afraid once I take her cherry, the pain will make her panic. I watch as she shyly reaches up to do as I ask. I kiss her chest, moving slowly to one of her breasts, tasting the flushed skin, nipping lovingly as I make my way to her nipple. "You're so beautiful Milen'kiy. You are everything I have ever dreamed of and more," I groan, letting my tongue lap against her hard, distended nipple.

"Niko," she whimpers.

"I'm never letting you go, Gabriella. *Never*," I vow.

"I never want you to," she cries as I suck the nipple deep, my tongue pushing it against the roof of my mouth.

I use my hold on her hips to push deeper inside She's so fucking hot...*slick*. It's so good but feels as if I'm in hell, because I am holding myself back.

Her fingers bite into my ass as she tries to pull me into her. Her head goes back against the pillow and her eyes close in passion. She doesn't understand what she needs, but she knows I'm the one that can give it to her.

And I will.

I can feel her orgasm begin. She's about to skyrocket. It's now or never. "Gabriella, I need you to open your eyes and look at me," I tell her. "Look at me," I growl when she fails to do as I ask.

Her eyes open quickly then, and the pleasure I see in them, steals my breath.

"My Niko," she whispers, and those words give me everything I need.

"I'm going to take you now, Milen'kiy. It's going to hurt, but it will get better. I want you to look at me. I want us to remember this moment forever."

"Okay," she whispers, but I feel her body stiffen.

"No, don't tighten up. I want to make this good for you. Just relax."

I slowly move from her body and then glide back in, shallowly riding her, not claiming her. I deserve a fucking medal, maybe even sainthood. I do this again and again, all while sucking on her nipples and playing with them. She's so wet that her sweet cream is dripping down my shaft and sliding against my balls. I watch Gabriella closely and I know before she even speaks that she's coming. It's there in the way her body is shuddering beneath me.

"I'm going to come. I'm going to…"

She moans out a breath that is so filled with pleasure that I know it will stay with me for a lifetime and even beyond. I can feel her climax roll through her and I know I have to finish this, because she's taking me with her and I'm going to come.

There's no holding back now.

My hold is bruising her hips, but I don't lighten it. I want my marks on her. I bite her nipple and she cries out from the pain her body trembling beneath me as I feel a gush of wetness as she comes even more with the added pain.

That's my moment. I choose it, claim it and slam inside of her, ripping away the barrier and claiming her virginity.

I hold myself still inside of her, despite the urgent need to fuck her.

"It's okay now," I croon. "You're mine now, Gabriella. I'm deep inside of you. Do you feel me?"

"Yes..." she says, her voice full of soft wonder. "It feels so good, Nikolai. We're a part of each other now."

That's all the reassurance that I need. I use my hold to teach her the rhythm we both need. She starts slowly, but soon she's meeting my every thrust. I suck on her tit again, my fingers moving between us to toy with her clit. She moves faster, as my thrusts grow more determined. I can feel her orgasm barreling back up, she's squeezing my cock so tight I can't breathe for the pleasure.

I can feel my cum begin to push through my body. I'm going to explode and when I do, I want to make sure she is with me. I grind my fingers against her clit, just as I thrust deep inside her tight body, and that's all it takes.

She screams out my name and comes hard, flooding my dick with her cum, flying apart in my arms. She throws her head back and cries, her nails scoring my skin and drawing blood. I've never seen anything more beautiful in my life.

I let myself go then, flooding her body with my cum, giving her everything I have.

"I feel you," Gabriella moans.

"Mine," I growl as I empty inside of her. "Milen'kiy!" My voice sounds more animal than man as I empty jet after jet of cum deep inside her fertile body.

Even when I'm done, I don't let go of her, I kiss her, needing that connection to tell her, without words, how special she is to me.

"And you're mine," she whispers, once we break apart, placing a gentle kiss against my chest that brands me as nothing else could.

19

GABRIELLA

"What if I'm dreaming?" I ask, my voice sleepy, my body feeling sore, but amazing.

After we made love, Niko moved me into the bathroom to soak in the tub, while he washed my hair and held me. I don't know what I expected, but the tenderness he gave me afterwards completely blew me away. If I had any walls left, they were totally obliterated by the sweet, gentle way he took care of me. It doesn't matter how quick this happened, it's clear that Niko cares about me, and I feel secure in that.

"If you are dreaming, Milen'kiy, then I definitely am and I hope neither of us ever wake."

"Me too," I purr, curling my body into him, craving the heat of his body close to mine.

"Are you okay, Princess?"

"I'm great," I assure him, blushing a little, because of the way he's looking at me.

"I meant, are you sore? I wasn't easy with you, I couldn't hold back like I needed to. You make me lose my head."

"I'm good, Niko. You were everything I have always dreamed

of and more. I wouldn't change anything about what we did together."

He kisses the top of my head and cradles me close. "You could be pregnant," he says. "Even now my child could be growing inside of you." His voice is hoarse as he puts his hand on my stomach, his eyes dropping down to watch his hand and my mouth goes dry.

I put my hand over his and squeeze.

"If I'm not now, then we'll keep trying until I am."

"You want my child? You don't want to wait?"

"Maybe I want you tied to me in every way possible too, Niko."

"I already am, Gabby," he laughs. "Still, I am in agreement with this plan. Does this mean you will marry me?"

"Absolutely, but not back in Georgia. I don't want my stepfather or my mother touching our wedding."

"Anything you want, Milen'kiy. I will give you the world, if you but ask."

"All I want is you—and our child," I respond grinning.

I'm rewarded when Niko growls, showing his pleasure in my statement by leaning down to kiss me.

The kiss is full of hunger, pleasure and love, making it kind of perfect.

Just like Niko.

He is perfect... *Perfect for me.*

20

NIKOLAI

Two Days Later

"I CAN'T BELIEVE you've never had a Christmas tree before, Niko," Gabby chastises.

I smile as I watch her scatter tinsel over the large nine foot, tree. I wanted bigger, but there was no time. Christmas is just a week away and I want my beautiful Princess to have the Christmas dreams are made of.

"I've never had a reason to celebrate holidays before you came into my life, Milen'kiy," I tell her honestly. She holds up the large star she purchased when we bought decorations earlier today. She takes a step toward me, and then goes on the tips of her toes to bring her lips to mine. I bend down to make it easier, and then take her kiss, deepening it.

"I know it's ridiculously quick, Niko, but I can't imagine being any happier than I am right now in this moment. You spoil me."

"You haven't seen anything yet, Gabby," I promise her and I mean every word of it.

"I would climb on the ladder, but I know you won't let me," she says holding out the star to me.

"You're right," I respond with a grin, grabbing another quick kiss from her lips.

I climb the ladder and place the star on top of the tree, straightening it. The jewels on it instantly begin reflecting with the blinking lights beneath. When I look back down at Gabby, I realize that the flickering lights are nothing compared to the shining of her eyes.

"It's perfect, Niko," she murmurs, looking at the tree.

"It is," I reply, but I'm not talking about the tree.

"I wish your brothers would have stayed for the holiday," she says, turning her attention back to me.

"They didn't scare you away?" I ask, only half joking.

"No," she giggles. "I was just starting to get used to them."

"I know one sure way to get them back for Christmas," I tell her, already planning it in my head.

"How's that?" she ask, her arms stretching to link around my neck as I hold her close. I slide my hand into my pocket, finding the box I put there earlier. I take it out, stepping away, flipping the lid open, as I look at her. She stares down at the princess-cut diamond and tears well in her eyes. "Niko?"

"Marry me, Gabby."

"It's too soon," she whispers, her gaze never leaving the ring.

"It's not. This is right, I feel it and I know you do, too. Marry me for Christmas, Milen'kiy."

"This is crazy," she says, finally looking up at me and I can see it on her face. She's going to say yes and my heart fills with pleasure.

"This is us. We were meant to be together, Princess. I knew it the first moment I saw you."

"You're sure this is what you want?" she asks.

I take the ring out and slide it onto her finger, then kissing her hand. "I *know* that you are what I want."

"Yes, Niko. I'll marry you," she murmurs, and I kiss her, tasting her lips which are salty from her tears. I don't want my Gabby to cry, but these tears are allowed because I know they are tears of happiness and that's my goal.

I am going to do my best to make sure that my Gabby tastes nothing but happiness for the rest of our lives.

EPILOGUE

NIKOLAI

Christmas Eve

"NIKOLAI! What are you doing? You're not supposed to see me before the wedding!"

"If you think that I can go one night without my Princess, you are insane. Besides, we don't need to rely on luck. We are going to make our own destiny," I tell her, as I slide into our bed.

"I don't really want to be away from you either, but I thought Victor was going to keep you out all night for your bachelor party and then crash at a motel on the main island."

"That was his plan, I never agreed to it, Milen'kiy. I'm not spending one night away from you."

"But, what about when you go on business trips? I won't always be able to travel with you, Niko. I'll have school and things here that need my attention, like our child."

"You can travel with me and when we have a child we can discuss it then. Are you sure that you're okay with moving here to

Greece permanently? You won't miss Georgia? What about going to the university there?" I ask, voicing the one worry I have.

"I love that you are willing to move there for me, Niko, but I love it here. I don't want to be near my stepfather. Besides, Greece is beautiful and your home is quiet and peaceful. It's the perfect place to raise a family. There's nothing keeping me in Georgia. I can finish my classes through the online study program. It's pretty easy now that I've switched my major to landscaping and design," she says and I love the excitement I hear in her voice. She's already showing me designs she's drawn of the garden and courtyard here. I've never done much with it, but the designs Gabby has shown me are beautiful and I love every change she proposes. Her stepfather is an idiot who doesn't know much of anything, but he was right about Gabriella's talent.

"As long as you're happy, Milen'kiy. That's all I want."

"I'm happy, Niko, and I can barely believe that tomorrow I will be Mrs. Nikolai Serepova. I feel like I'm a fairytale princess," she says and giggles. I squeeze her tight.

"I'm not sure I qualify as a prince in our fairytale, Gabby, but you are most definitely my Princess."

"You are my prince and one day when I tell our daughter the story of how I was rescued from the evil ogre, you will most definitely be the star."

"We could have a son you know."

"Either way," she laughs.

"I do like the sound of this," I tell her kissing along the side of her neck.

"What?" she moans, tilting her head to the side to give me access.

"You're talking about having a child with me. Now I just have to keep trying to get you pregnant. Not that I mind. You know what they say, Milen'kiy."

"What's that?" she asks, her hips thrusting up as my hand slides between her legs.

"Practice makes perfect," I rasp against her skin, letting my teeth make small teasing nips on her tender flesh as I kiss my way down to her breasts.

"I like the way you practice, Niko," she mumbles, as she kisses down my chest, sliding out of my grip. I don't fight her, because she's sliding down and then throws a leg over me, settling herself so that she's astride me. My cock pushes up against her warm, wet entrance and I groan at how fucking good it feels.

"Take me inside of you, Gabby," I literally beg, thrusting up against her wet depths. I can feel the juices from her pussy run down against my shaft. She's so wet and ready to be fucked and I'm hard as nails, my balls already so heavy that it's painful. She positions me at her entrance and then slowly slides down on me, not stopping until I'm deep inside of her, filling her body. The muscles of her pussy are quivering around my cock, encircling it and flexing to hold me tightly inside of her and my eyes close from the pleasure. "Milen'kiy," I groan, my eyes opening up to look at her.

My woman.

My life.

My love.

"Niko," she breathes, leaning down to bring her lips to mine.

My fingers bury into her hair as I hold her mouth to mine, kissing her with all of the emotion I feel inside.

"Milen'kiy," I whisper against her lips.

"It seems impossible," she puffs out, riding me. "This has happened so quickly."

"To me it feels as if it has taken way too long for you to become mine. I can't wait until tomorrow when you say, I do."

"I love you, Niko," she says, giving me the words for the first time. Words that until this moment, I truly thought were inconsequential. Love seemed a pale way to describe the woman who breathes life into my world. Yet, hearing her proclaim her feelings for me feels so fucking good that I know I will want those words from her for the rest of my life.

Still, if she gives me that, then I need to give her the same.

"And I love you, Gabriella. I will love you in this world and whatever comes in the next one. I will love you always," I vow and then I stop talking, because Gabriella begins moving faster and all rational thought flees as I make love to my woman. Tomorrow is Christmas and she will become my bride, but I know that she is already my soulmate. Tomorrow will only be the first Christmas of many. Perhaps this time of year is the season of miracles.

I definitely have one in Gabby.

EPILOGUE

GABRIELLA

One Year Later

"THERE ARE times in a man's life when he has to just stop and thank God for the life he's been given, Milen'kiy. When I come home from work and find you curled up on the couch holding our daughter, I feel the urge to get down on my knees and thank the Man upstairs."

I smile, my heart overflowing.

My life with Niko is better than anything I could have dreamed. We still live in Greece and I don't see me ever wanting to leave. Since the birth of our daughter, Nicolette, Niko has fixed it so he handles most of his work here through conference calls and Skype. On the occasions where he is needed in the corporate offices, he always makes sure he's home within a couple of days. Neither of us handle separation very well. Maybe that's not healthy, I don't know, but I do know I never want it to change.

"I should have her in her crib, but your brother Victor has stolen her all day. Other than feeding her, I've barely gotten any time with her. I'm so glad you're home. How did the office search go?" I ask as he walks over to kiss me.

Our lips barely touch, but it's enough for now. Then, he's bending into me even farther so that he can kiss our daughter's soft, black curls. My heart squeezes as I see the way he loves our child. I couldn't have asked for a better father for our little Nikki.

"Victor is here?"

"Yes. He said he just wanted to check on you, but we both know it was to see the baby." She's barely doing more than sleeping and crying for food at this point, but she already has her father and three uncles wrapped around her little finger. Victor is as fascinated as Niko by her. I heard him telling Niko the other night that he's tired of being single. He's thinking of agreeing to an arranged marriage. I'm worried about him, but I haven't said anything. Victor is as headstrong as Niko—all of the Serepova brothers are. I doubt they would listen to me at all, at least about this.

"He's trying to steal moya doch'," Niko grumbles.

"As if anyone could steal your daughter. You know she's Daddy's little girl," I laugh, loving the way he refers to our daughter in Russian. Actually, anytime Niko uses Russian it excites me. He took notice of it, of course, and now always makes sure to use that language when referring to me--especially when we are making love.

I'm a really, *really* lucky woman.

"Where is Victor? I'd like to try and talk him out of this foolishness of agreeing to an arranged marriage, at least one more time."

"What happened to the man who once thought there was nothing wrong with that?" I laugh.

"He met the love of his life," he tells me, kissing me again, before sitting beside me on the sofa and brushing his finger across our daughter's hair. He's staring down at her with so much love that I'm not sure my heart can take it.

"Victor is in the study, but Niko, maybe you shouldn't talk him out of it?"

"How can you say that, Milen'kiy? Do you not want my brother to find love like we have?" he asks.

"I do, but you have to admit that our marriage didn't start off the most convential way. Perhaps he'll find the woman he's meant to have through this marriage?"

"But what if he doesn't?" Niko asks, obviously worried.

"Didn't you tell me that you knew I was the woman that was meant for you after just one look?"

"I did. It felt like being struck by lightning," he says with a smile that warms his dark eyes.

"Then, try getting Victor to agree to calling the marriage off if he doesn't have similar feelings after meeting her."

"You talk as if you think Victor is rational," he jokes, but some of the worry fades from his face.

"I think all you can do is try and ultimately your brother will have to make his own decisions, moy muzh."

"Your Russian is improving, Princess."

"I have a very good teacher and he rewards me when I get a word right."

"How about you put our daughter down for her nap and meet me in our bed for another lesson?"

"I really like that plan," I respond, grinning, my body already growing warm from the thought of making love with Niko.

"Good. I'll be right there, I just want to have a brief word with Victor."

"Don't keep me waiting. I need you too much," I warn him, as he gets up from the sofa and starts walking to the study. He stops and looks at me, flashing me a devastatingly handsome grin.

"The feeling is very much mutual, Milen'kiy. *Very. Much.*"

The sinful grin on his face as he says those two words are enough to make my ovaries explode. I watch him walk away, as my thoughts replay my life with him. A little over a year ago, I let Nikolai Serepova into my heart and somehow each and every day just gets sweeter and sweeter.

I look down at my beautiful daughter. I hope one day, she finds a man as wonderful as her father. I'm going to urge her to never settle, because even if Niko doesn't believe it, he is my prince and I want the same exact fairytale for my daughter.

She deserves a happily ever after, just like the one I have with her father. A life full of love. And that's exactly what I have thanks to the bossy Russian business man who once saw me from afar and didn't stop until I agreed to let him claim me.

It's the best fairytale ever.

The End.

ALSO BY L. NICOLE

The Billionaire's Christmas Bride

The Billionaire's Purchased Wife

Her Dirty Billionaires

ABOUT THE AUTHOR

L. Nicole loves to write about Alpha men who have one thing and one thing only on their mind—their women. She creates stories with alpha men who will stop at nothing to claim the woman they love.

If you want to stay in touch with Lily you can find her on Facebook!

Author Page

Made in the USA
Las Vegas, NV
08 March 2022

45247955R10052